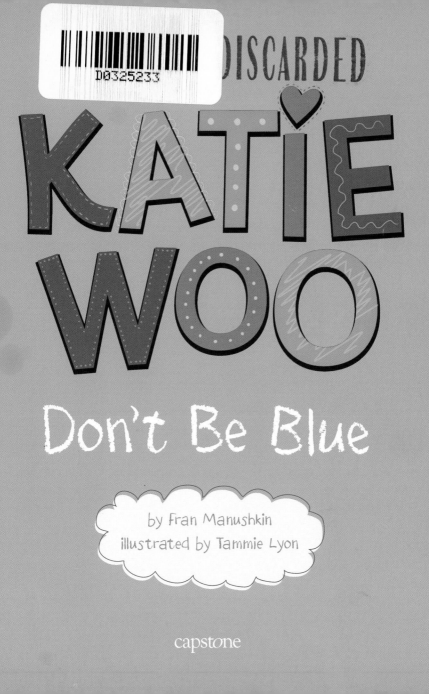

KATIE WOO

Don't Be Blue

by Fran Manushkin
illustrated by Tammie Lyon

capstone

Katie Woo is published by Picture Window Books
A Capstone Imprint
1710 Roe Crest Drive
North Mankato, MN 56003
www.capstonepub.com

Library of Congress Cataloging-in-Publication Data Manushkin, Fran.
Katie Woo, don't be blue / by Fran Manushkin; illustrated by Tammie Lyon.
    p. cm. -- (Katie Woo)
Summary: In these four previously published stories Katie learns to cope with
situations she finds unpleasant.
ISBN 978-1-4048-8101-3 (pbk.)

1. Woo, Katie (Fictitious character)—Juvenile fiction. 2. Chinese Americans—
Juvenile fiction. 3. Chinese American families—Juvenile fiction. 4.
Emotions—Juvenile fiction. [1. Chinese Americans—Fiction. 2. Family life—
Fiction. 3. Emotions—Fiction.] I. Lyon, Tammie, ill. II. Title. III. Title: Katie
Woo, do not be blue. IV. Series: Manushkin, Fran. Katie Woo.
 PZ7.M3195Kbg 2013
 813.54—dc23   2012029162

Photo Credits
Greg Holch, pg. 96; Tammie Lyon, pg. 96

Designers: Emily Harris and Kristi Carlson

Printed in the United States of America in North Mankato, Minnesota.
032017   010318R

Table of Contents

A Nervous Night

Katie Woo was going to a sleepover at Grandma and Grandpa's house.

She packed her suitcase. Then she kissed her mom and dad goodbye.

Katie climbed into the car.

"I'm so glad you moved close to me," she told her grandparents. "Now I can sleep over a lot!"

When Katie saw the house, she smiled. "It's a little house in a big woods," she said.

"It's cozy," said Grandma. "You'll see."

Katie put her suitcase in the guest room. It didn't look cozy at all.

The bed was too big, and the walls were a yucky color.

"Come and plant some tomatoes with me," said Grandpa.

Outside, Katie dug holes and dropped tiny seeds in them.

"In the summer, we'll pick the tomatoes together," Grandpa promised.

Inside, Katie helped Grandma
make wontons.

"The next time you visit," said
Grandma, "we'll make noodle soup."

"This house is fun," Katie said.

"Indoors and out!" said Grandma. "From our porch we can see the sunset."

"And when you come in the summer," said Grandpa, "you will see shooting stars."

"It's bath time!" called Grandma.

"Hey," Katie said, "this tub has legs. Are you sure it won't walk away with me?"

"I'm sure," said Grandma.

"You never know," said Katie.

After her bath, Katie put on her pajamas.

"I don't like this bed," Katie decided. "It's too high. What if I fall out?"

"This is your mother's old bed," Grandma said. "She never fell out."

"Really?" said Katie. "Being up so high *does* make me feel like a princess."

"And our home is your castle," Grandma said with a smile.

"This castle is a little spooky right now," Katie told Grandpa.

"Don't worry!" he told her. "We have a night-light."

"Yikes!" Katie yelled. "There's a bear in my castle."

"That's just the shadow of your mom's old teddy bear!" said Grandpa.

"Right! I knew that!" said Katie.
She grabbed the teddy bear and
hugged him tight.

"Would Princess Katie like some cookies?" offered Grandpa.

"I'd like to call Mom," Katie decided.

"Mom!" said Katie into the phone.
"You forgot your teddy bear. Maybe I
should come home with it now."

"That's okay," said her mom. "You
can bring it back tomorrow."

"Katie," said Grandpa, "I wish you'd stay. I made your favorite — ginger cookies."

"And I will sing your mom's favorite lullabies," Grandma added.

Katie's mom told
her, "Nobody sings
lullabies like Grandma!
I miss them — and
Grandpa's cookies, too."

"All right!" Katie decided. "I'll
stay."

After cookies and milk, Katie
snuggled under the covers.

"In the summer," she told Grandma
and Grandpa, "we will eat tomatoes
and make noodles and see shooting
stars!"

"I'm coming back — for sure!"
Katie told the teddy bear.

And she dreamed of shooting stars all night.

Too Much
Rain

One day it started to rain. It rained all day, and it rained all night.

"When will it stop?" Katie Woo asked her mom.

Katie's mom told her, "The weatherman says it will keep raining until tomorrow."

The mayor was on TV.

"There may be some flooding," he warned. "Everyone should go to a shelter. When the rain stops, you can go home."

Katie packed a suitcase with shirts and pants and underpants and pajamas.

She also took her teddy bear and her cat Sweet Pea's bowl and mouse toy.

"I want to take along our family photo album," said Katie's mom. "It has all the pictures of us with Grandma and Grandpa. I thought it was in the living room. But I can't find it."

Katie helped search for the album.

But nobody found it.

The family had to leave without it.

As they drove away, Katie saw water flooding into her neighbors' houses.

It was scary!

The shelter was in the high school gym.

Katie's friends Pedro and JoJo were already there.

JoJo was holding her little cat, Niblet.

"Niblet was hiding in the closet," JoJo said. "We almost had to leave without her."

That night, Katie slept on a cot at the shelter. Many other people did too.

The shelter felt strange to Katie.
She hugged Sweet Pea and her teddy
bear tight.

The next morning, the mayor said, "I have good news! The rain has stopped. Everyone can go home."

Katie Woo was worried about her house. Would it be flooded with water?

Katie's family hurried back to their house.

When they reached their block, Katie saw her house standing tall!

A stream of water was pouring out of the basement window.

Katie spotted something floating in the water.

"Mom!" Katie shouted. "It's our photo album!"

Katie's mom hurried out of the car and grabbed the album before it floated away.

"The cover is wet, but the pages are okay," she said.

The family was so happy to be home!

They made hot chocolate and drank it in their warm kitchen.

"There is some water in the basement," said Katie's dad. "But we can pump it out."

Katie called her friends JoJo and Pedro. Their houses were safe, too.

"We were lucky," said Katie's mom.
"We have our house, and we have each
other."

"Let's take a happy picture for our photo album," Katie said.

So they did!

Moving Day

Katie's family was moving.

"You will love our new house," said Katie's mom.

"I like this one!" said Katie. "Why can't we stay here?"

"Your mom has a great new job," said Katie's dad. "We want to live close to it."

"Who will get my old bedroom?" Katie asked.

"Another girl like you," said Katie's mom.

"I will write her a note," Katie decided.

"Dear new person," she wrote. "I hope you like this room. I loved it so much! Sincerely, Katie Woo."

The Woo family drove away.

Katie's dad said, "Our new bathroom is great. It has a whirlpool bath."

"A whirlpool?" thought Katie.
"What if I spin around and around
and never stop?"

"Our new house has a sunken living room," said Katie's mom.

"Uh-oh," thought Katie, "what if I sink down into the floor and disappear? This house sounds weird!"

Suddenly, there it was! The new house!

"It doesn't look spooky," thought Katie. "But you never know."

Katie peeked into the living room. "It's not sunken!" she said.

"No way!" Her dad smiled. "It's called 'sunken' because it's a few steps down."

"Very fancy!" said Katie.

In the bathroom, Katie asked, "Where's the scary whirlpool?"

"It's not scary," said her mom. She turned on the whirlpool.

"Wow!" Katie said. "It's great for bubble baths!"

Suddenly, they heard a loud
wailing. It was coming from the attic.

"Oh no!" Katie yelled. "This house
is haunted!"

Then a girl came running into the house. She raced upstairs.

Seconds later, she came down, holding a puppy.

"My puppy escaped from his travel box and hid in the attic. We almost left without him!" the girl said.

"I'm so glad you didn't," said Katie.

Katie went to her bedroom to unpack.

Outside her window, she saw birds building a nest. "You are my new neighbors," Katie said with a smile.

Soon, Katie smelled something wonderful.

"Mom is making wonton soup!" she said.

Katie heard pretty
music too.

"And Dad is playing
the piano." Katie smiled.
"This place is starting to feel like
home."

As the family ate supper, Katie
wondered, "Where's my bed?"

"I don't know," said her mom. "The
store said it's coming today."

"I can sleep in the whirlpool bath," Katie teased. "It might be cozy, but my blanket will get very wet."

Just then, the doorbell rang, and in came Katie's bed.

"It's a bunk bed!" she yelled. "I can have sleepovers with Pedro and JoJo."

At bedtime, the moon shone into Katie's room. It lit up a piece of paper in the corner.

It was a note! Katie read it.

"Dear new girl, I hope you like this room. I did! A lot!"

"I love it!" Katie decided.

"Good night, new room!" she chanted, and she fell asleep.

Katie Woo
Has the Flu

"Ah-choo!" said Katie Woo.

"Bless you!" said her mom.

"Ah-choo!" Katie sneezed again and again and again.

"I feel funny," said Katie. "But not in a fun way. My tummy hurts, too."

"Uh-oh," said her mom. "I think you have a bug."

"Ugh!" said Katie. "I don't want bugs running around in my tummy."

"Not that kind of bug," said her mom. "A flu bug."

"Good," said Katie. "But I still feel bad."

"I feel hot, too," Katie moaned.

Her mom took her temperature.

"You have a fever," Mom said.
"That's why you feel so hot. No school
today! You are going back to bed."

"I feel so hot, I might melt!" Katie
moaned.

"Don't worry," her mom assured her.
"You're not ice cream. You won't melt."

"I'm so glad!" said Katie.

Soon Katie began to shiver. "How can I feel cold and hot at the same time?" she wondered.

"The flu is tricky," said her mom.

"That's a sneaky trick," said Katie.

Katie's mom gave her pills to take. "Yuck," Katie groaned. "Pills are such . . . pills."

Katie fell asleep and had a bad
dream. She dreamed she was a polar
bear who lost her fur. She shivered
and shook!

When Katie woke up, her mom read her a story. It was about a girl with hair so long, she could jump rope with it.

Her dad sang her a happy song.

Katie drew a picture of the flu bug

flying away from her.

Katie's mom brought her hot soup and toast.

"Ew, soup!" Katie moaned. "Ew, toast! I'm not hungry."

Later, JoJo called Katie. "I missed you today! Miss Winkle says it's not the same without you."

"Thanks," Katie croaked.

"Ribbit!" JoJo croaked back. Katie
smiled.

Then Pedro
called. He told Katie,
"When I broke my leg,
everyone wrote funny
things on my cast."

"Lucky you," said
Katie. "There is no cast with the flu."

She drew a picture of everyone
writing their names on her arms.

"That would tickle," Katie decided.

Katie took another little nap.
When she woke up, she felt a lot
better.

Her mom brought her more soup and toast.

"Yay, soup!" Katie said. "Yay, toast! I'm starving!"

"I'm feeling more like me," Katie said. "It feels good to feel good!"

That night, Katie dreamed that her class sang a "Welcome Back" song to her.

Miss Winkle played the tambourine and did a happy dance.

A few days later, Katie went back to school. Her friends welcomed her with a song.

"Boo on the flu," they sang. "We missed you!"

"I did too!" sang Miss Winkle.

Katie sang back: "I feel like new! Like a new Katie Woo!"

And it was true!

Having Fun with Katie Woo!

Bugs on a Log

In *Katie Woo Has the Flu*, Katie thought she had bugs running around in her tummy! If you eat this great treat, you could have bugs in your tummy, too.

What you need:

- a butter knife
- 2 celery stalks, cut in half
- 1/3 cup peanut butter
- 1/4 cup raisins

What you do:

1. Using the butter knife, fill the hollows of the celery with peanut butter.
2. Place raisins (or bugs) on the peanut butter.
3. Enjoy!

Become a chef and experiment with different
ingredients. Here are some ideas you can mix and
match.

Instead of peanut butter, use...

- cream cheese

- cheese spread

- hummus

- tuna salad

- tofu dip

Instead of raisins, use...

- chocolate chips

- marshmallows

- sunflower seeds

- peanuts

- pine nuts

- diced carrots

- currants

A Brown-Bag Bird's Nest

In *Moving Day*, Katie watches a bird build a nest outside her window. You can make your own nest with this fun project.

What you need:

- a brown paper lunch bag
- craft glue
- dried leaves, grass, and flowers
- optional: a bird and eggs from a craft store

What you do:

1. Open up the paper bag. Pull the bottom of the bag up toward the top. As you do this, the sides will crumple. Work with your bag to make it into a bowl shape.

2. Apply some glue to the bag, then stick a leaf on it. Repeat until your bag is covered with leaves. You can also glue on flowers or other lightweight items to decorate your bag.

3. Fill the bag with dried grass. If you would like, add a bird and eggs. Now you have a nest that looks as great as the real thing! Set it on a shelf or table for a pretty decoration.

About the Author

Fran Manushkin is the author of many popular picture books, including *Baby, Come Out!*; *Latkes and Applesauce: A Hanukkah Story*; *The Tushy Book*; *The Belly Book*; and *Big Girl Panties*. There is a real Katie Woo — she's Fran's great-niece — but she never gets in half the trouble of the Katie Woo in the books. Fran writes on her beloved Mac computer in New York City, without the help of her two naughty cats, Chaim and Goldy.

About the Illustrator

Tammie Lyon began her love for drawing at a young age while sitting at the kitchen table with her dad. She continued her love of art and eventually attended the Columbus College of Art and Design, where she earned a bachelors degree in fine art. After a brief career as a professional ballet dancer, she decided to devote herself full time to illustration. Today she lives with her husband, Lee, in Cincinnati, Ohio. Her dogs, Gus and Dudley, keep her company as she works in her studio.